10/05

GHJ

WHITNE... OF AMER... ADMIT ONE · 263011 · NATIONAL TICKET CO.

5 SKEE BALL 5 COUPON · ASBURY CASINO · Asbury Park, N. J. · 804126 · NATIONAL TICKET CO., SHAMOKIN, PA.

CAMP · COUPON CHECK · 5 · 35156

N · CENTER · 108 · ROW · SEAT · ORCHESTRA $28.00 · MINETTA LANE THEATRE · GOOD ONLY · SAT. 10:00 P.M. · NOVEMBER · 24 · 1984 · NATIONAL TICKET CO., SHAMOKIN, PA.

CORONET · Arcade Theatre · ...MIT ...NE · ADMISSION $5.00 · ...KET CO., SHAMOKIN, PA. · 236989

121501

D1469434

National Design Museum
Smithsonian Institution
Cooper-Hewitt
...t Street
...Y 10128
68
HOURS
Tuesday 10:00 – 9:00 PM
Wednesday–Friday 10:00 – 5:00 PM
Saturday 10:00 – 5:00 PM
Sunday 12:00 – 5:00 PM
GENERAL ADMISSION
121501

Lincoln Theatre 1 & B'way · PATRON'S RECEIPT · $5.00 · ADM. PRICE · 171425 · 171426 · 171427

ONE · 50¢ · TICKET · GLOBE TICKET COMPANY · 000817 · 8000

Child · World Trade Center Observation Deck

5948
GEN. ADMISSION $10.00
MADISON SQUARE GARDEN
108th YEAR
WESTMINSTER KENNEL CLUB SHOW
GOOD EITHER DAY
FEB. 13 AND FEB. 14, 1984
NO RETURN CHECKS
ARGUS-SIMPLEX BROWN, INC. N.Y.C.

DISCARDED

NEW YORK CAT SHOW
No 11520

80 St. Marks ...rks PL., N.Y.C. · MISSION $6.00 · ...KET CO. N.Y.C. · 77807

SOUVENIR OF VISIT TO THE MOST FAMOUS BUILDING IN THE WORLD · EMPIRE STATE OBSERVATORIES · 295715

4108R B5 10-79
PROPERTY OF
NAME
STREET
CITY _____ STATE
TELEPHONE ( )
THIS IS NOT A BAGGAGE CLAIM CHECK

THE CITY OF NEW YORK
DEPARTMENT OF TRANSPORTATION
STATEN ISLAND FERRY
(S.I.-N.Y.)
SMALL VEHICLE
PRESENT BOTH PARTS AT GATE
PART 2 RETAINED BY DRIVER
No 011514

Vehicle Use Permit · NEW YORK STATE · Parks, Recreation and Historic Preservation · $5.00 · 2000 · APR 07 2001 · Date · NOT REFUNDABLE · 879609

CAMP · COUPON CHECK · No 10678 C · NOT GOOD IF DETACHED · 10 CENTS

...ADMIT ONE · 4¢ · 4¢

Loews 83rd St. · NEW YORK CITY · Patron's Receipt · 1 · ADM. · Incl. Taxes · 5.00 · REVOCABLE AT WILL OF MGT. · 010020 · 010019 · 010018 · NATIONAL TICKET CO.

Loews 83rd St. · NEW YORK CITY · Patron's Receipt · 1 · ADM. · Incl. Taxes · 5.00 · REVOCABLE AT WILL OF MGT.

Summerpier · August 27, 1983 · THE DAVID AMRAM QUINTET · ELLIOTT TICKET CO. N.Y.C. · 001206

World in Wax MUSEE · Henderson Block, Coney Island · ADMIT ONE · 20 · EST. PRICE ... TOTAL · FED'L TAX 03¢ · 20¢ · 082218

CAROUSEL · MANAGED BY THE MAKKOS ORGANIZATION · GOOD FOR ONE RIDE · 002116 · NATIONAL TICKET CO., SHAMOKIN, PA. 17872 U.S.A. 570-672-2900

NASHVILLE PUBLIC LIBRARY

for sweet and saucy Clementine, the real dog.

J.

VIKING
Published by Penguin Group
Penguin Young Readers Group, 345 Hudson Street,
New York, New York 10014, U.S.A.

Penguin Books Ltd, Registered Offices: 80 Strand, London WC2R 0RL, England

First published in 2005 by Viking, a division of
Penguin Young Readers Group

1 3 5 7 9 10 8 6 4 2

Library of Congress
Cataloging-in-Publication data is available
ISBN: 0-670-05929-3

Manufactured in China
Set in Walbaum

gorge on Gnocchi
by GLADYS

Clementine
in the
CITY

by

Jessie

HARTLand

VIKING

Not so very long ago...

I lived in a
TEENY-WEENY house
on a PINT-SIZED lot
on a QUIET LITTLE street
in a MINUSCULE town.

All the dogs I knew

slept all day

or chased squirrels

or cats.

There was not much else for a dog to do.

Because life in the town was such a bore,
everyone watched way too much TV.

And the food was not what I would call tasty!
Limited choices. Not even Chinese takeout.

No variety of shops, either.
One of this, one of that.

If dogs worked at all, their jobs were dull.
They might mow lawns, fold laundry, or
be hired to bark at things.

One day I spotted an interesting ad in the paper.
The Big City Circus was looking for a poodle to star
in a new act.

"I'M GOING TO GET THAT JOB!"

So I packed up all my stuff:

my red scooter,
my candy collection,
my map rack,
my microscope,
and thirteen globes.

My friends tried to talk me out of going.
"You're not a circus dog!"
"The city is a dangerous place!"
"Don't go."
But I left the small town anyway . . .

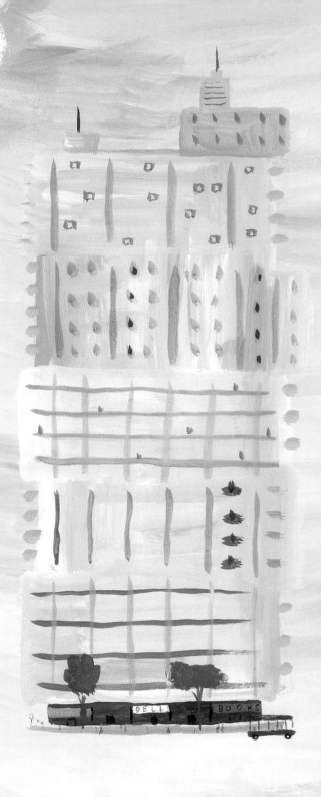

and moved to

an ENORMOUS building

a whole block LARGE

and fifty stories HUGE

on a WIDE and *lively* avenue

in the

big BIG CITY.

My name is Clementine.

This is my story.

Cars honking. Buses beeping. Everyone in a hurry.

First morning in the big city and I rush over to the circus where a harried hippo takes one look at me and snaps, "What can you do?"

"Well," I say, "I'm learning how to juggle."

"I want to see more," says the hippo. "A costume . . .

a unicycle . . .
a bit of razzle-dazzle, some fluff.
Shop for your props; practice,
practice, PRACTICE; and report back
in three days for opening night."

What's a POODLE to do?

Only three days to get ready for my big circus debut. Where to start?

Unpack.
Work on my act?

Grab a map.
Go!

HAVE a snack.

BLINTZ MOBILE

HOT Pretzels

falafel

CHINESE
Dumplings

menu

HOT DOGS

shish KEBAB

CHOCO
CHOCO
CHOCO

KITS

BON BONS

CANDY

SAM'S HATS

Miso Softy

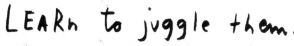

Buy 3 hats.

LEARn to juggle them.

Find a pack.

"Where, oh where," I ask my new pack of friends, "do you go on a damp drippy day when you're all juggled out and there's no place to play?"

ZILLIONS of places!

UPTOWN! to the museum district.

At the MODERN ART MUSEUM,
I learn that if the eye is on the cheek,
it must be a Picasso.

DOWNTOWN! to see a show.

Broadway Theatre
CONVENTION CTR
BOAT SHOW
off off B'way
SHOW
CAT SHOW
VILLAGE
VANGUARD
LIVE MUSIC
FLEA CIRCUS

In the MUSIC DISTRICT I learn
that if the instruments are:
    a washboard,
    a double bass,
    oodles of horns,
    and a bunch of clamshells,
it must be JAZZ.

Here's the candy of choice in the city:

nutty jazzy! gridlocked
BROADWAY
chock-full lively! jam-packed

MY circus debut is in two days.
I've got my three hats but I still need:
 a unicycle,
 a trumpet,
 and a feather boa.

3 hats ✓
UNICYCLE
feather BOA
trumpet
tray with food?
small skirt?

Where can I go
to get my
feather boa?

Clementine

The FEATHER DISTRICT!

That's where you go when you want feathers.
So that's where I go.

A SHINY new MORNING. The sun is hot. And only one day until my debut. I have to lick my act into shape, and . . . *ding dong* my friends are here! "Come with us, Clementine, you can practice on the beach!"

I wonder if the subway train goes to the sea?

It does!

That's where you go when you want to cool off.
So that's where we go.

I learn that old boots make fine
boats for itty bitty kitties.

WHERE
do you go when
you want some new boots?
Settle for something humdrum
in the only shoe store
in a town?

NO!
You can
walk all over
the big city, go to 534 shoe stores,
and try on 187 pairs of boots until . . .
you have the jazziest, snappiest, grooviest boots around.

SOME NIGHTS in the city after jazzy, snappy, busy days, you are in your apartment on the 47th floor and you are tired. You can have dinner delivered! Rawhide bits, shark fin soup, dried pig's ears, gnocchi, Wiener schnitzel, cheese blintzes, even haemool soondooboo. You name it.

"WOW! Where did you get those boots?"

"WOW! Where do you get your hair done?"

Fancy city dogs with fancy city tastes have many choices:

This GIANT schnauzer is

having a massage.

CAROLA is having

her portrait painted.

This AIREDALE is

enjoying AROMATHERAPY.

Punch visiting the doggie bakery—

for the second time today.

BRUNO swimming laps

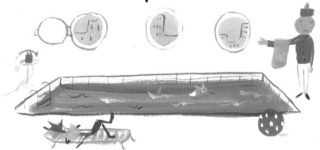

at a dog LAP POOL.

"But," I ask her,

"where do you go if you don't have a lot of dough?"

"Your friends can wash you at a special place
called The Launder Mutt."

A bright new day.

The air is CRISP.
My boots are NEW.
My hair is COIFED.
My boa is FLUFFED.

Tonight is my opening night
at the circus!

How do you get to work when
you live here and work there?
SCOOT to the bus,
BUS to the tram,
TRAM to the ferry,
FERRY to the subway,
SUBWAY to the taxi,
TAXI to the circus.

That's how I go.

On an INKY night
under a SAGGY tent
I make my circus
debut.

There is a DRUM ROLL as the curtain parts.

I ride out on a unicycle, holding a tray of cheese blintzes while playing a trumpet and juggling three hats.

It was the hardest thing I ever had to do.

CRASH! BOOM! BANG! I fell.

Fortunately, in the big city there is a hospital just for animals.

ANIMAL MEDICAL CENTER

Emergency Room

CANINE
Ambulance

ANT
AMBULANCE

SQUIRREL
AMBULANCE

It's just a broken arm. I'm no circus dog!

Maybe I should have stayed in the small town.

Sulking in the bed next to me is an EVEN grumpier dog with a broken leg.

I cheer him up with my big city tales:
He GIGGLES at the grooming,
GUFFAWS at the kitty in my boot,
SNICKERS at the feathers,
and CHORTLES at all the shoe shopping.

"Clementine, you're just the dog I've been looking for! You moved here from a small town only three days ago and already you know the city so well.

"How would you like to write stories for my new travel magazine?"

BACK I GO,
THROUGH the Feather District,
OVER the bridge,
PAST Groomerama,
the art museums,
and all the shows . . .

to my enormous building a whole block long, fifty stories huge . . .

to pack it all up

and head for my first travel assignment:

TOKYO!

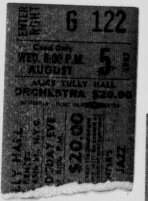

ENTER RIGHT
G 122
Good Only
WED. 8:00 P.M.
AUGUST 5
ALICE TULLY HALL
ORCHESTRA $20.00

8th St. Pla
B018725
ADM ON
$5.

NATIONAL TICKET CO.

ADMIT ONE
0774799

ADM. PRICE $4.00
PATRON'S RECEIPT
001871

YOUR NUMBER
61
WHEN CALLED IT'S YOUR TURN FOR SERVICE
PRINTED IN U.S.A.

0139861

American Museum of Natural History

MB
The Museum of Broadcasting
1 East 53 Street
New York, New York 10022
NATIONAL TICKET CO., SHAMOKIN, PA.

004057

LOEWS SHOWPLACE
N.Y.C.
Patron's Receipt
2 ADM. Incl. Taxes 6.00
039926
REVOCABLE AT WILL OF MGT.

THEATRE
ay, N.Y.C.
ONE
ON 2.00
(S) 260
036487

MTA MetroCard
← Insert this way / This side facing you

Carnegie Hall
FRANK SINATRA
SEPT. 82
PARQUET
22
2652
Price $50.00
S 113

WED. EVE.,
Price $50.00
CARNEGIE HALL
57th St. and 7th Ave.
WED. EVE., SEPT. 22, 1982
Programs & Artists subject to change
No Refunds - No Exchanges
Latecomers will be seated at the discretion of management

PARQUET
S 113

WORLD TRADE CENTER OBSERVATION DECK

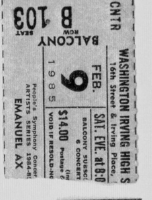

CNTR
BALCONY
SEAT B 103
ROW
WASHINGTON IRVING HIGH S
16th Street & Irving Place,
FEB. 9 1985
EMANUEL AX
People's Symphony Concert
ARTISTS SERIES 1984-8
$14.00
BALCONY SUBSCI
& CONCERT
SAT. EVE. at 8:0
VOID IF RESOLD-N
Postage 2

TICKET
604198

MADAME TUSSAUD'S
NEW YORK
VALID ON 11/26/00 ONLY
SPEED COMBO
Madi Exhibition & Second Gate

Adult
World Trade Center Observation Deck

TUE
28 JAN 1986
WELCOME TO
LATE NIGHT
WITH
DAVID LETTERMAN
PERSONS UNDER 16 NOT ADMITTED
DOORS 5:10 PM
CLOSE

NEW YORK STATE THEATER
NEW YORK CITY BALLET
The Nutcracker
SUNDAY EVENING
NOV 29, 1998 5:00 PM
Right
Fourth Ring
F 30
NEW YORK STATE THEATER
LINCOLN CENTER PLAZA
BROADWAY AT 63RD ST. NYC
$25.00
98110652 991129E

SOUTH STREET SEAPORT MUSEUM

RAIN CHECK
Price incl. 8½% tax
NEW YORK YANKEES
vs Montreal Expos
YANKEE STADIUM
BX 314
TUE JUN 12, 2001 7:05PM

BA1105E
EVENT CODE
32.00
PRICE & ALL TAXES INCL.
CONVENIENCE CHARGE
SEC 1
SECTION/BOX
CA 37X
ROW
A 10
SEAT
19
BAC603
19OCT9

SEC 1 A 10 GROUP
SECTION/BOX ROW SEAT All Taxes Incl. If Applicable
CENTER MEZZANINE 32.00
TJ MAXX PRESENTS
BIG APPLE CIRCUS
LINCOLN CENTER
HAPPY ON
BROADWAY & W 63RD STREET
THU NOV 5, 1998 6:30PM